CATCH THAT WOBBUFFET!

Adapted by Tracey West

Scholastic Inc.

New York   Toronto   London   Auckland   Sydney

Mexico City   New Delhi   Hong Kong   Buenos Aires

ISBN 0-439-53051-2

12 11 10 9 8   7 8/0

Printed in the U.S.A.
First printing, March 2003

Ash and his friends, Brock and Misty, were walking in the woods.

"*Pika! Pika!*" said Pikachu. Ash's Electric Pokémon saw something on the path.

Two strange people stopped them.
"This is our new Poké Pod,"
said one. "We want to try it out.
Can we use your Pikachu?"

The strange people took Pikachu.
They put Pikachu in the Poké Pod.

Then they took off their glasses and coats.

"Team Rocket!" Ash cried.

"We tricked you," said Jessie.

"Now we have your Pikachu!" said James.

Team Rocket ran off with Pikachu.

Team Rocket had a plan.
Jessie gave Pikachu to her Wobbuffet.
Then Wobbuffet ran away.

But Wobbuffet fell into the river.
    The blue Pokémon let go of Pikachu.
    Ash caught Pikachu just in time.
    "Now open this Poké Pod right now!"
Ash told Team Rocket.

"The Poké Pod will not open without a key," Jessie said.

"Then give me the key," Ash said.

"We can't," Jessie said. "Wobbuffet has the key!"

"Catch that Wobbuffet!" Ash cried.

Wobbuffet floated down the river.

Ash and his friends ran after Wobbuffet.

Team Rocket chased Wobbuffet, too.

Thump! Wobbuffet bumped into a Quagsire.

"*Quagsire*," said the Water Pokémon.

Quagsire showed Wobbuffet how to get to land.

Wobbuffet got out of the water.
It climbed up a tree.
It held on to a vine.
It swung from tree to tree.

Everyone chased Wobbuffet through the woods.

They ran down a hill.

"Where is Wobbuffet?" Ash asked.

"Wobbuffet is up there!" Jessie cried.
A tree branch stuck out of the hill.
Poor Wobbuffet was hanging from the branch.

Zoom! A truck came speeding down the road.

Wobbuffet fell. It landed on the truck.

Then Officer Jenny drove up.

"Step aside," she said. "We have to catch that truck!"

A thief named Ganef is in that truck,"
Officer Jenny said.

"We have to catch the truck, too," Ash
said. He told her about Wobbuffet.

"Get in fast!" Officer Jenny said.

Ash and his friends got into the
police car.

The police caught up to Ganef.

"I will get away in my balloon!" Ganef cried.

But Wobbuffet got in the balloon first!

Everyone watched Wobbuffet fly away.

Team Rocket got in their balloon.

They chased after Wobbuffet.

Wobbuffet jumped into Team Rocket's balloon.

But Wobbuffet broke the balloon by mistake!

Wobbuffet fell to the ground.

Ash called on his Chikorita.

"Chikorita, use Vine Whip to catch Wobbuffet!" he cried.

Chikorita grabbed Wobbuffet with its vines.

Wobbuffet landed in a speedboat.
The boat zoomed down the river.

Ash ran down one side of the river.

Team Rocket ran down the other side of the river.

Then Ash and Jessie jumped into the speeding boat.

Ash and Jessie could not stop the boat.
Wobbuffet flew out of the boat.
"Come back, Wobbuffet!" Jessie
yelled.

The boat was about to crash into a bridge.

"Totodile, I choose you!" Ash yelled.

Totodile used Water Gun to slow down the boat.

Ash and Jessie landed safely.
Officer Jenny ran up to Ash.

"Ganef the thief got away again," she said. "He is in that old building. And Wobbuffet is with him!"

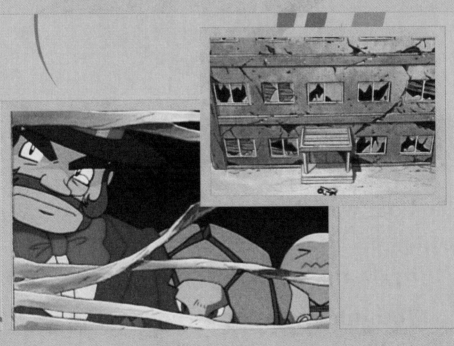

Inside the building, Ganef and Wobbuffet were not alone.

Ganef called on his Golem. Golem is a super tough Rock Pokémon.

Team Rocket dug a tunnel. They got into the building.

"Hand over that Wobbuffet!" James cried.

"Golem, go get them!" Ganef yelled.

Ash and Totodile ran through the tunnel.

Ash saw Golem attacking Team Rocket.

Totodile hit Golem with Water Gun.

Golem fought back.

Golem tried to tackle Totodile.

But Wobbuffet used a move called Counter.

Golem and Ganef crashed through the wall.

"We have you now!" said Officer Jenny.

Team Rocket took off with Wobbuffet in a new balloon.

"Oh no!" Ash cried. "Wobbuffet still has the key!"

"Pika!" said Pikachu.

Ash called on his Noctowl.

"Peck a hole in that balloon!" he cried.

Noctowl pecked away. Air shot out of the balloon.

The key fell from Wobbuffet's neck. It landed in Ash's hand.

Ash got Pikachu out of the Poké Pod.

"*Pika . . . chuuu!*" Pikachu hit Team Rocket with Thunderbolt.

"We are blasting off again!" Team Rocket wailed.

"Thank you for helping us catch the
thief," Officer Jenny told Ash.

"We're just happy that Pikachu is out
of that Poké Pod," Ash said. Misty and
Brock hugged Pikachu.

"*Pika!*" Pikachu agreed.

A toast!

 for everyone!

CHOCOLATE   MILK

Hip, hip, hooray!

Now the  and

LADY IN PINK   HENCHMAN TYRONE

want to be good guys!

"I will save you!" I say.

So I save the  .

LADY IN PINK

Oops!

The  syrup is falling!

The is falling too!

The  says
LADY IN PINK

the   is hers!
CHOCOLATE   MILK

All hers!

She opens the .
CONTAINERS

She finds a ,
GLASS

, and syrup.
MILK CHOCOLATE

The secret is !
CHOCOLATE MILK

Not so fast!

The  LADY IN PINK has  MISS T. !

The  LADY IN PINK says,

"Hand over the  CONTAINERS !"

No problem!

My 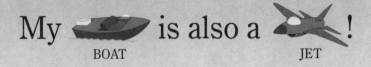 is also a 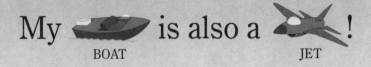!

BOAT JET

I jet away.

Now I have all **3** !

THREE CONTAINERS

At the ISLAND

I grab secret CONTAINER THREE 3.

Uh-oh! The LADY IN PINK again!

 appears in the .

MISS T. SNOW CONE

She sends me to an .

ISLAND

Now I zoom to the . BEACH

I walk into a  bar. JUICE

I order a . SNOW CONE

No problem!

My 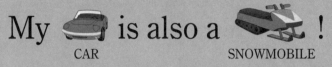 is also a !

CAR   SNOWMOBILE

I get away again.

At the Dairy
FARM

I grab secret  **2.**
CONTAINER TWO

Uh-oh! The  !
LADY IN PINK

The hot dog is really a .
PHONE

 is on the .
MISS T.   PHONE

She sends me to the Dairy .
FARM

I zoom to the .
MOUNTAINS

I get a .
HOT DOG

No problem!

My  is also a .
CAR   HELICOPTER

I get away!

I zip to the Glass  .

BUILDING

I grab the  .

CONTAINER

Uh-oh! The  !

LADY IN PINK

The  and

LADY IN PINK   HENCHMAN TYRONE

are the bad guys.

MISS T. appears in the  **BANANA** split!

She gives me a clue.

Secret **CONTAINER** **ONE** 1

is in the Glass  **BUILDING**.

I zoom to the  CITY in my CAR.

I stop at an ICE CREAM shop.

I order a BANANA split.

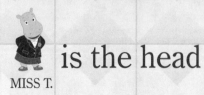 is the head

of the spy agency.

 will give me clues

to help me find the .

CONTAINERS

I have to find **3** secret 🔫🔫🔫.
THREE   CONTAINERS

1 is in the 🏛️.
CONTAINER ONE   CITY

2 is in the 🏔️.
CONTAINER TWO   MOUNTAINS

3 is at the 🏖️.
CONTAINER THREE   BEACH

Hello, I am .
AGENT SECRET

I am a Super Spy.

Library of Congress Cataloging-in-Publication Data
Inches, Alison.
Super spies / adapted by Alison Inches ; based on a teleplay
written by Robert Scull ; illustrated by A&J Studios. — 1st ed.
p. cm. — (Ready-to-read)
"Based on the TV series Nick Jr. The Backyardigans as seen on Nick Jr." — T.p. verso.
ISBN-13: 978-1-4169-3825-5
ISBN-10: 1-4169-3825-7
I. Scull, Robert. II. A&J Studios. III. Backyardigans (Television program) IV. Title.
PZ7.I355Stw 2007
[E]—dc22   2007014289

Super Spies

adapted by Alison Inches
based on a teleplay written by Robert Scull
illustrated by A&J Studios

Ready-to-Read

SIMON SPOTLIGHT/NICK JR.
New York   London   Toronto   Sydney